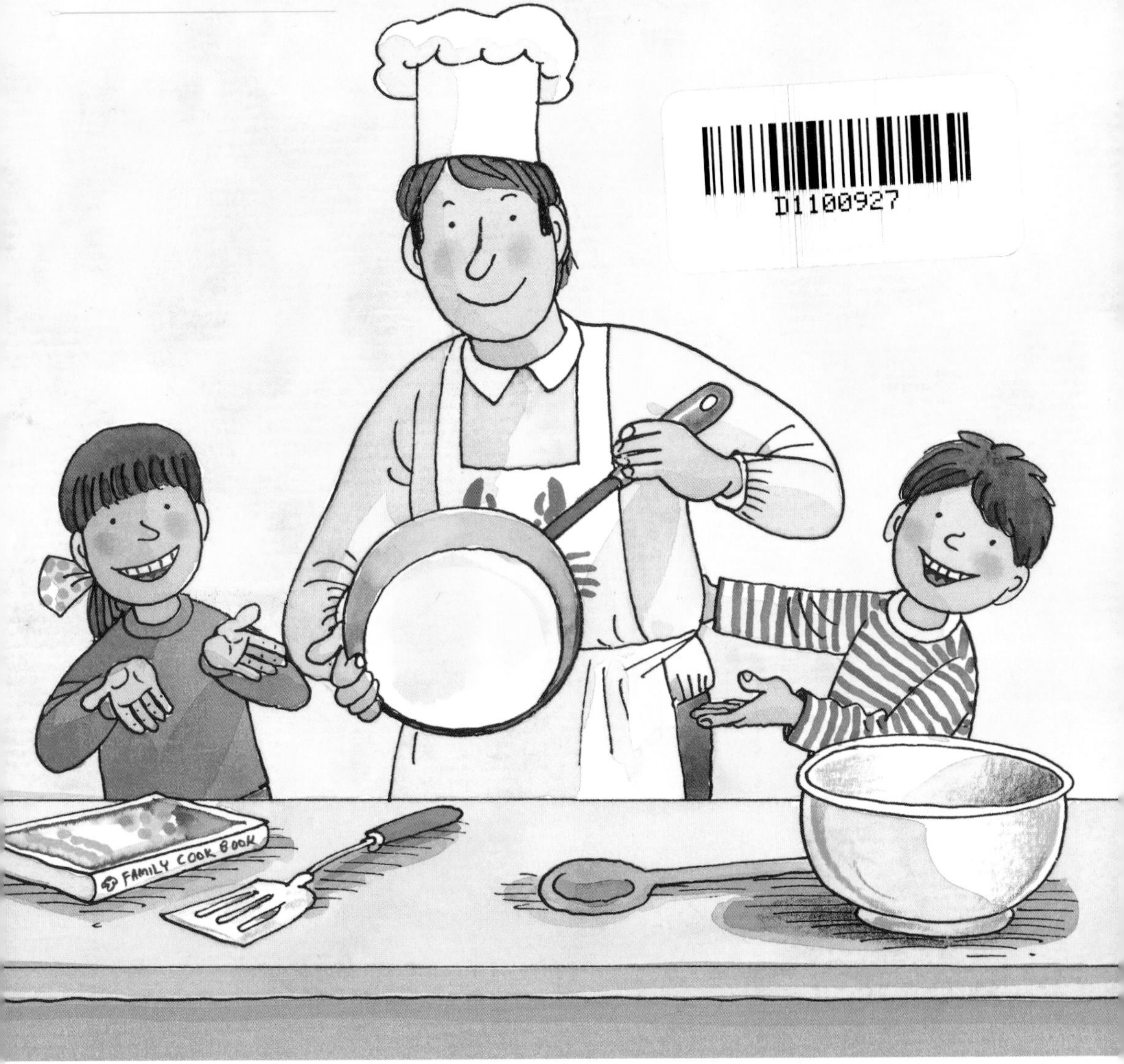

The frying pan,

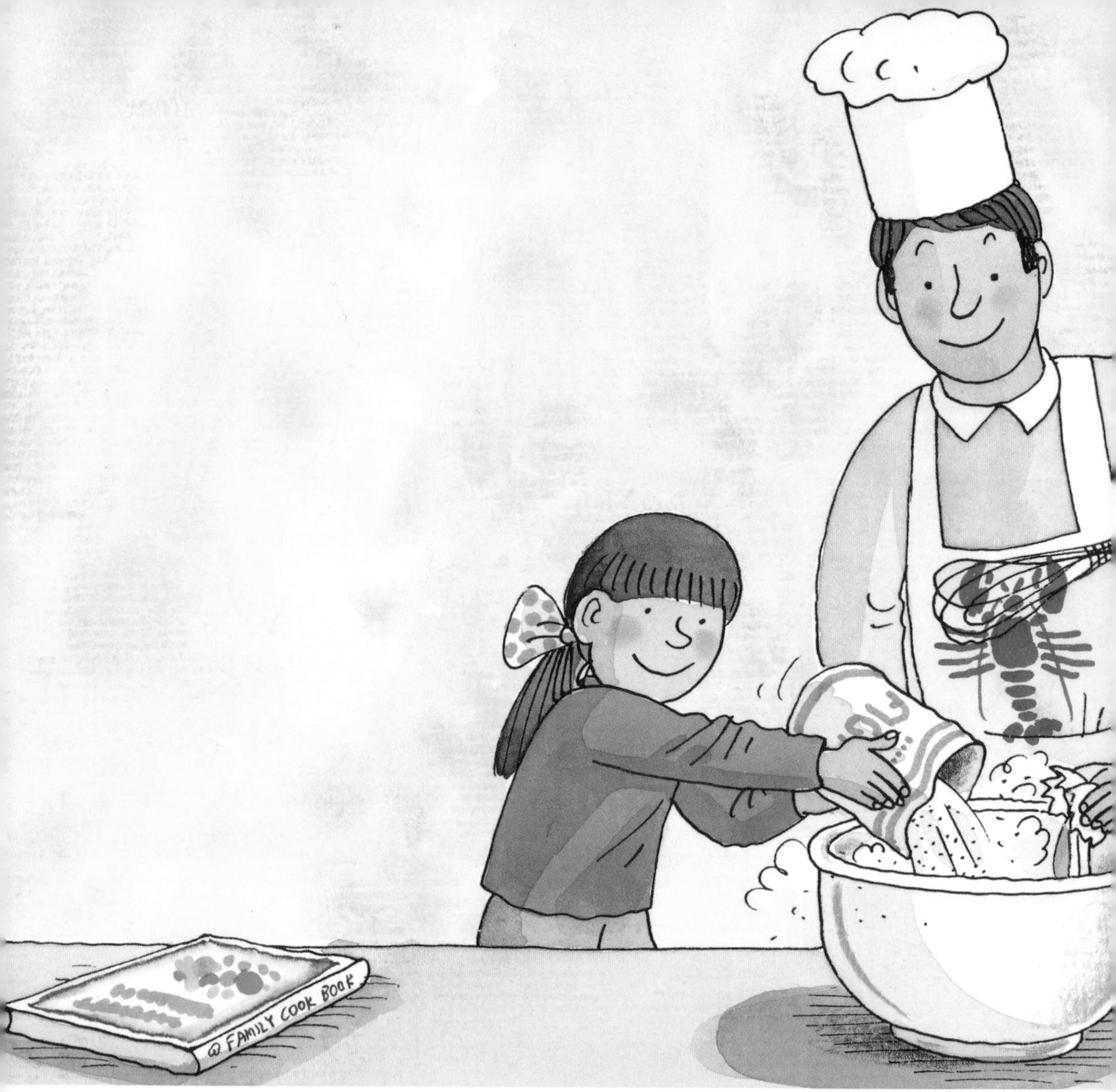
FAMILY COOK BOOK

the flour,

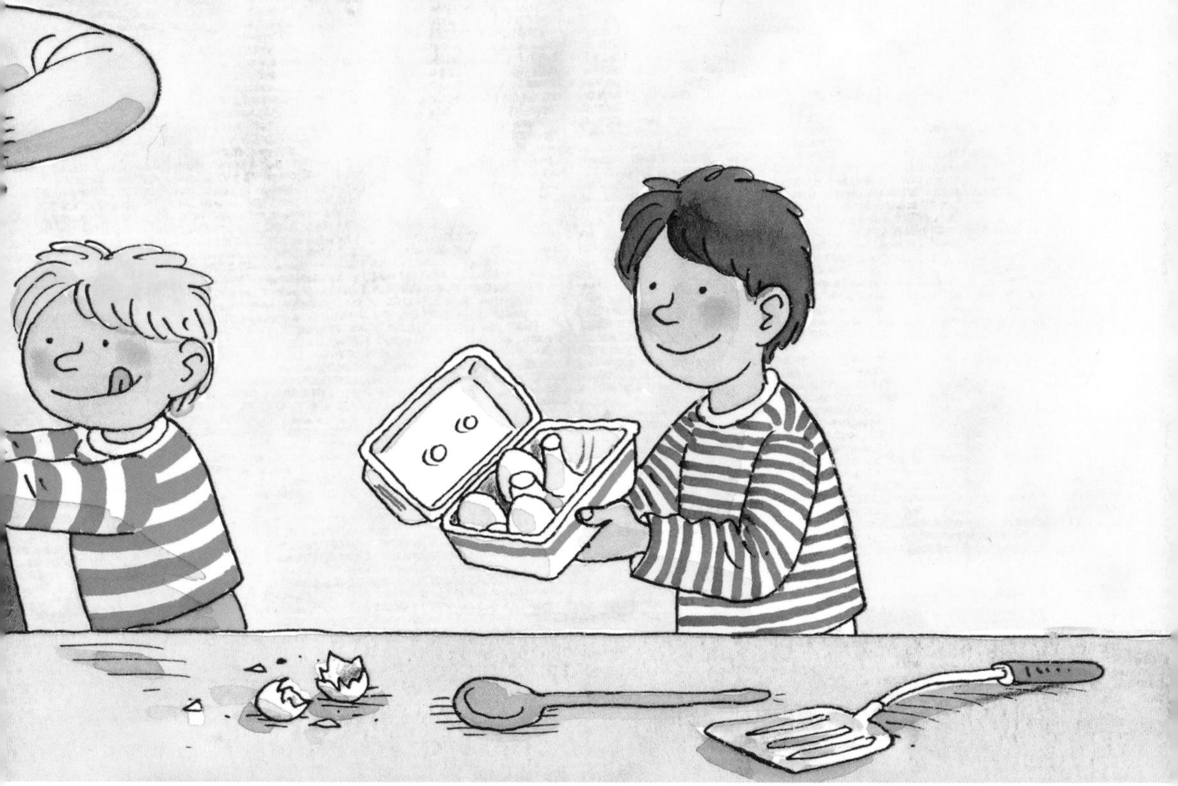

the eggs,

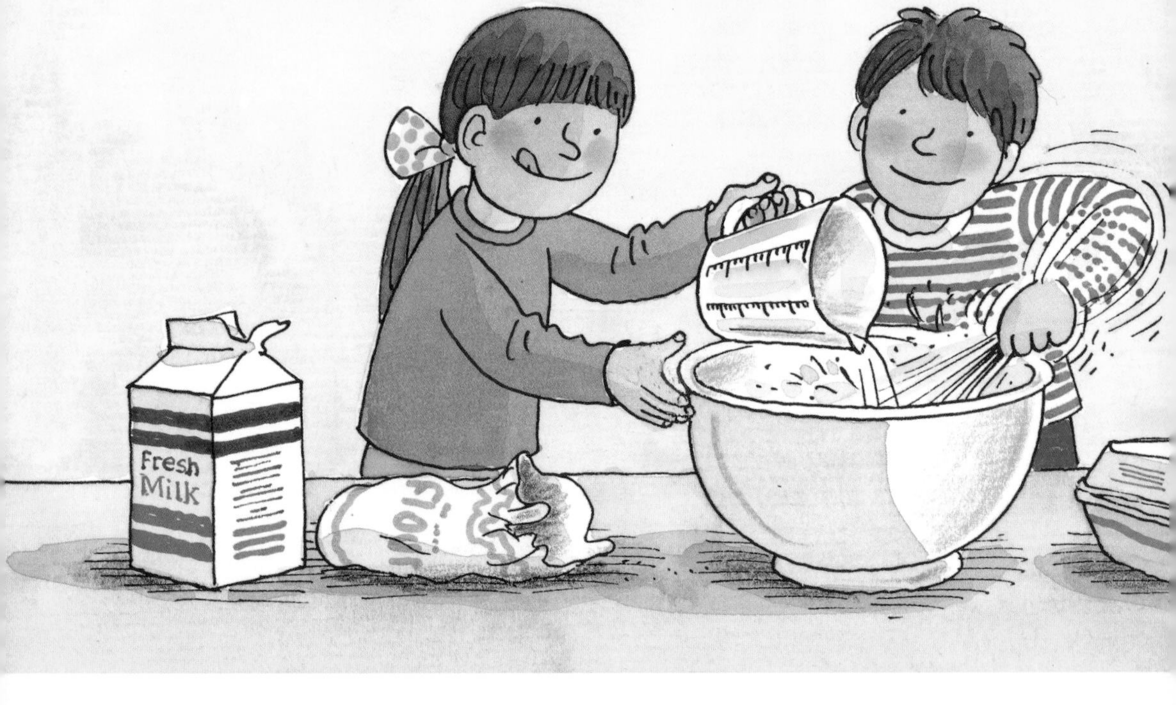
Fresh Milk
Flour

the milk,

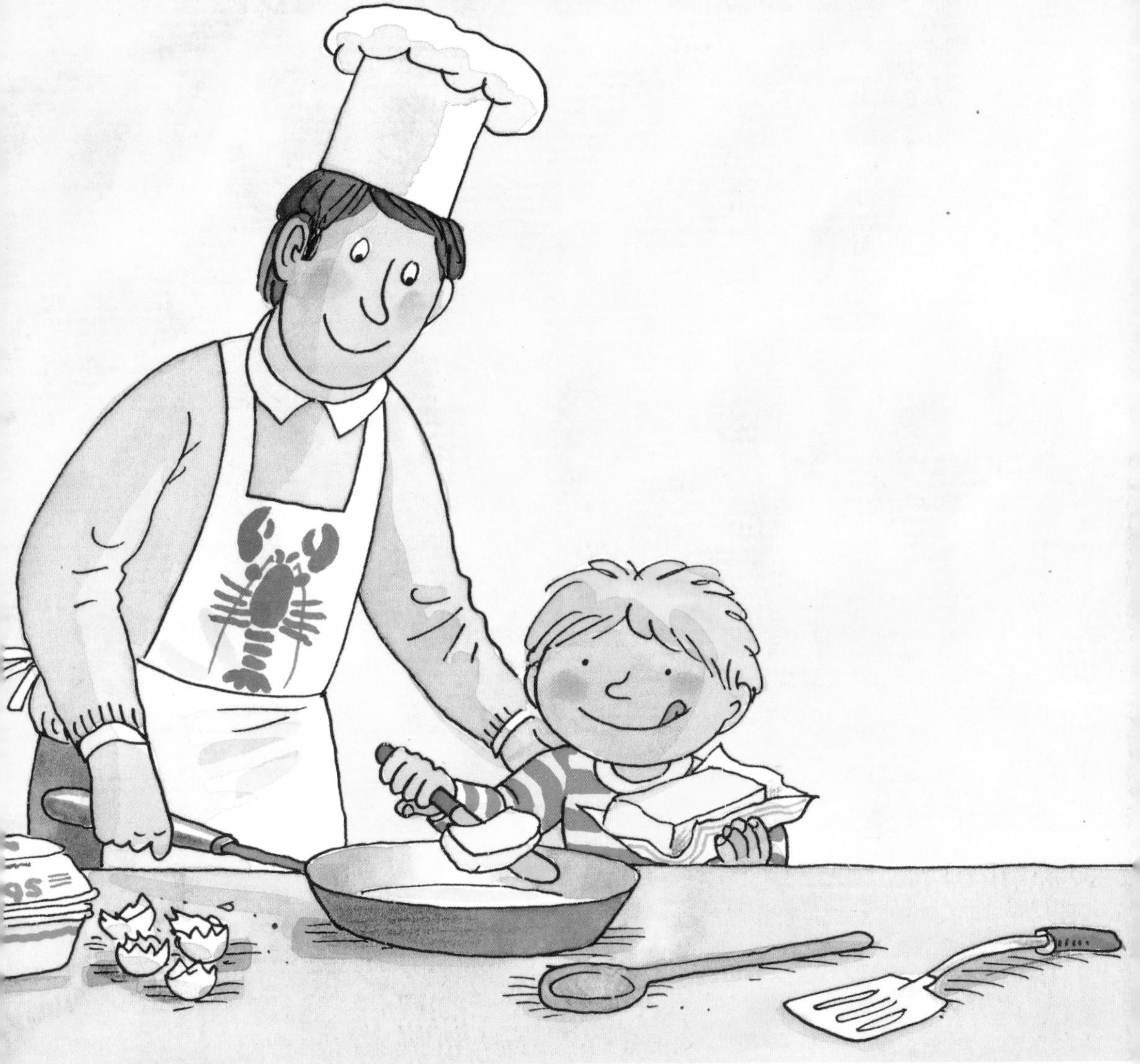

the butter,

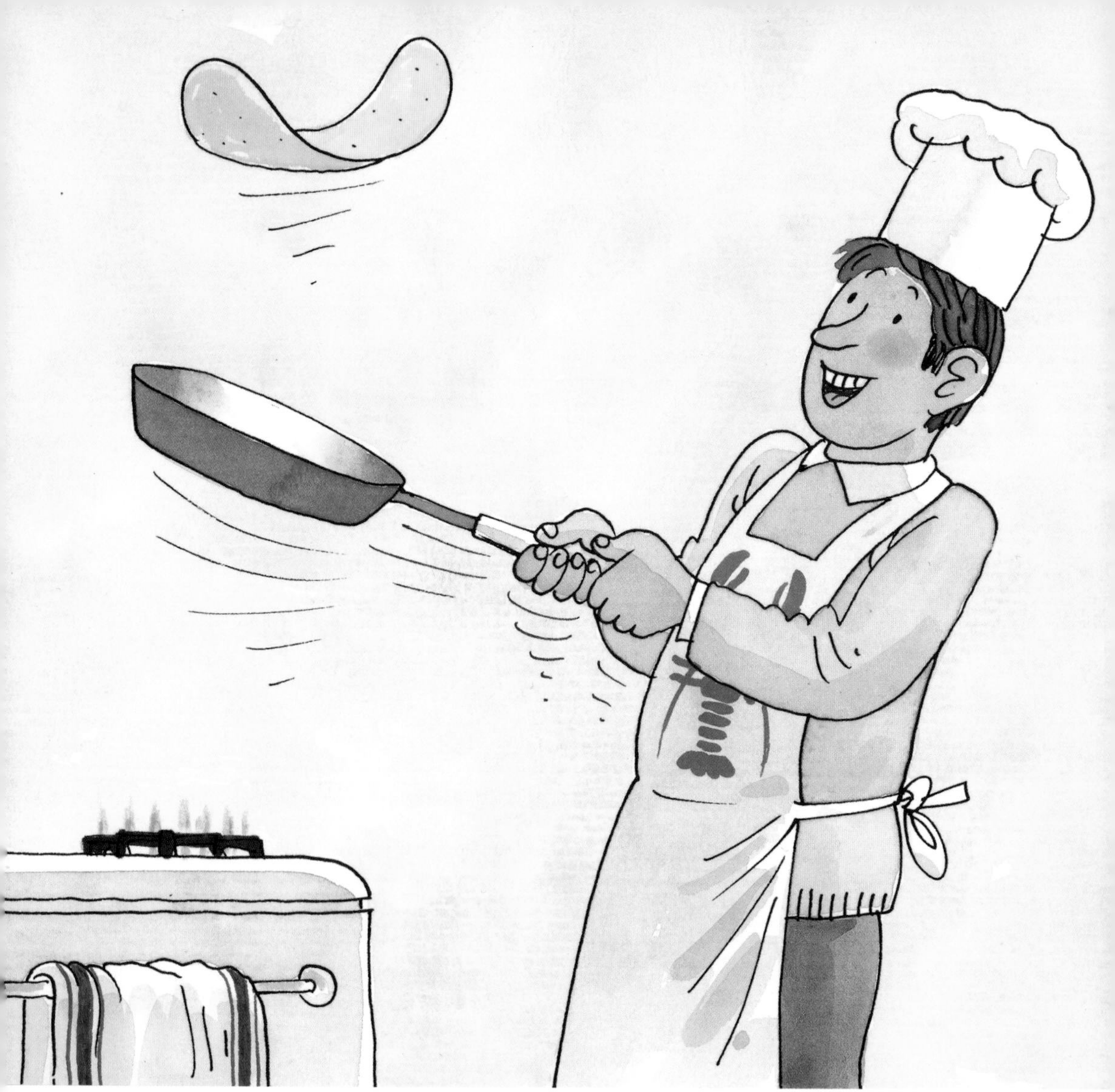

the pancake,

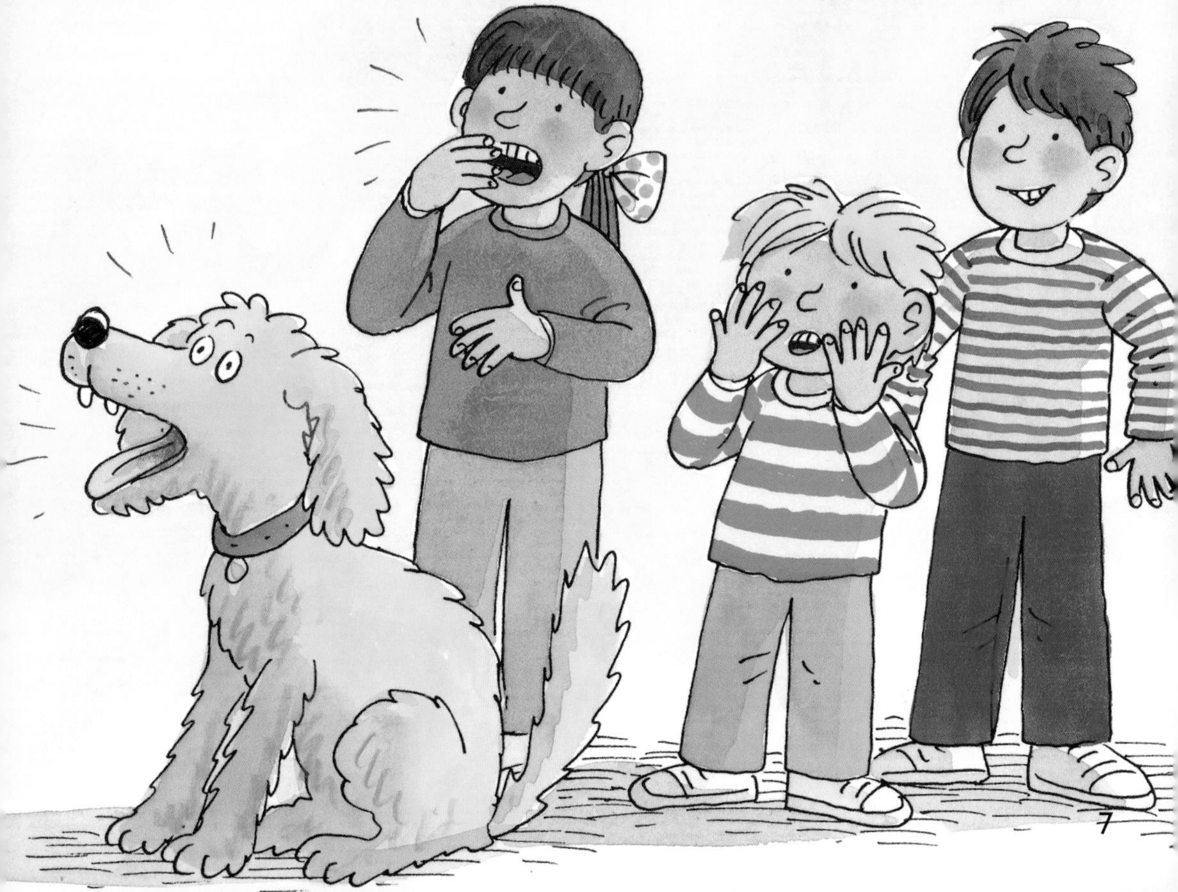

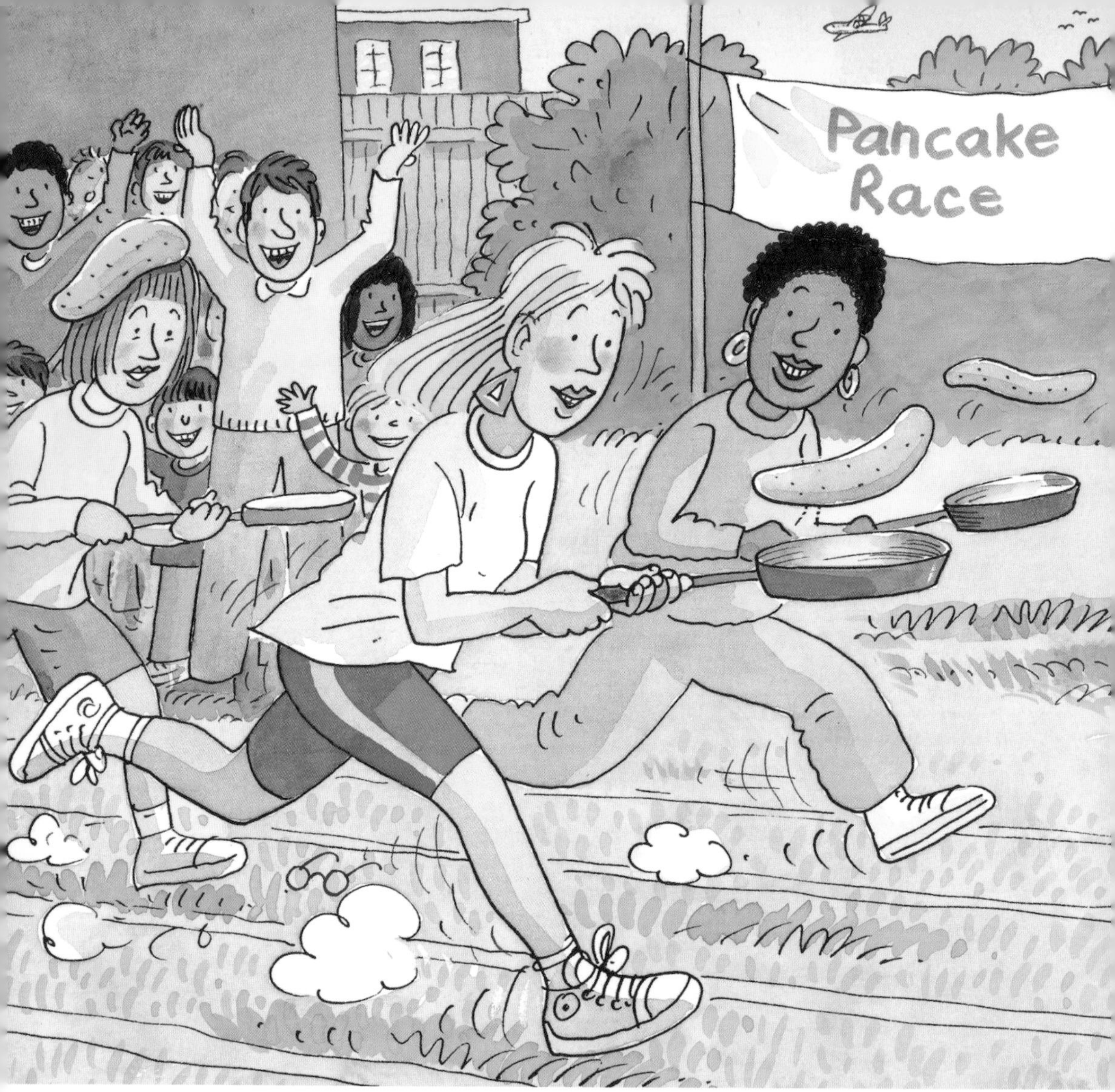

the pancake race.